CREEPY STREET

HAFSA SADIYA HK

ISBN 979-888591891-6

First and foremost, I'm grateful to Almighty for showering his blessings.

Contents

Foreword

My first book "One Night" is fiction based and the whole plot relates to the girl flying in the sky and coincidently even for the second book the plot relates to the kids experiencing the ocean and I realized this,when I was nearing the completion of this manuscript. I'm always fond of thrilling stuff and I love to keep the readers on the edge of the seat and I hope they enjoy the roller coaster ride.

Preface

Pandemic has taken a heavy toll on all of us and lockdown has unlocked my potential to explore at the fullest. I got plentiful time to put my pen to paper for these crazy fiction stories. Since it's only online school, at times I feel lethargic due to lengthy screen time but mum's expressions reminds me to keep focused and continue my writing journey.

This time I hired an illustrator...Guys just kidding, It's my buddy RithuPranaa, 8th Grade from Chettinad Vidyashram School, Chennai. I can count on her as she patiently managed my insanity and portrayed my imagination in the form of art.She has done the whole illustration and showcased her artistic skills, I can't stop myself to say she is the BEST ILLUSTRATOR.

Acknowledgements

I extend my heartfelt thanks to my family and friends for their valuable reviews and I earnestly request you to give me the honest feedback which will help me to improvise and do the best for my next endeavor. I can't express my joy on how exciting it would be to read the reviews and I'm looking forward to it.

I owe huge thanks to my teacher Mr. Ashadh who corrected my silly mistakes and my sincere regards to Unity Public school which has been very supportive and shaped me to achieve this milestone.

Bunch of Thanks to Abdur Raziq for giving me an opportinty to place my first book at his book store in Grand Mall, I owe them a lot.

A big thanks to Mr Vignesh from Tardiverse who helped to launch book in Metaverse,So guys grab your VR set and catch the glimpse of it.

My heartful thanks to all the lovable readers of my first book "One Night" without whom I'd have never got this motivation and the courage to sail through this bumpy journey. Mom and Dad as always keep encouraging me to explore the unexplored and I owe them everything. This book would never have been completed without my Mom's constant reminders. She takes care of all the other things so I can focus more on my creative work and pen down my thoughts.

Here are the reviews of my first book.

"Nice read , While I definitely recommend this book to other readers, I would recommend it to young kids, mainly because it will resonate better with them." -Afzal

"The book was awesome
Like Dreamy night"-Mohammed Jiyavudeen

"This book is the excellent book I have never seen. usually I am a book worm and love to read books. this book is the perfect one for bookworms. so blindly go for it.
I recommend it firmly. and also it is written by a 12 year old author and so a big applause for her. super awesome book. loved it"-Asshabha

"This book is amazing and it worths a read...It is very comprehensive and creative. The author's imagination makes the story fascinating. The best part is it is written by a 12 year old author. A round of applause for this fiction story..."-Mohammed Azeem

"This book is amazing and worth a read. Kids will enjoy reading this. If you have interest in fictious stories then don't miss it."-Kiran

"The children love the story line and the humour in this book. I choose this rating because the book intrigue me and made me want to read more. I would recommend this to people who love fiction stories"-Aneesur Rahaman.

"The book was freaking awesome that too the last part was soo niceeeeeeeee .
A 12 year old kid wrote this book cant imagine frankly !
Very good book you people can get for you kids believe me its niceee."-Ryas

"The best book for kids...Easy vocabulary, easy to grasp and keep me interested. Keep going Author...looking forward for many more books"-Manjari

"Book is really interesting.. language used in the book is very light and easily understandable .....it takes u into the characters forgetting self"-Asma

"Awesome book... Loved it. Awesome book by a 12 year old author. Simple and easy language for children. Keep going "-Siva

"A great story. You all should read it. It is meaning full to read and the sentence is formed very nice. I wish you post again a story."-Shannawaz

"This book is easy to read and understand for kids. The word use in this book is really interesting and children love this book."-Mohd quasim.

"I really liked this book Go for it guys it is more interesting and easily to understand good job hafsa waiting to see many more books "-Bhavya

"Absolutely loved the songs interwoven in the story and end of Marty waiting on Tina's terrace. Good work by Hafsa"

"Had never imagined a 12 year old writing such an awesome book. Good luck in writing more like this book."-Shehzeer

"Good Story and very comprehensive please try to read out and review from your side as i did to encourange"-Jaleel

"Fantastic"-Shabbir

Prologue

We were gasping for air, when we reached the top hill. We four were panting and exhausted.

I was searching for Addison to quench my thirst as the water bottles were in her backpack. That's when I realized Addison was missing. I was shattered when I realized it!! And I was trembling to tell it to Jackson.

"Umm.. Jackson I think we missed Addison while we were climbing" I said tremblingly.

"You are joking aren't you?! Where could she go? Should be here only lets search!" he

said in a shivering voice.

Jackson is not a person who can stay strong, he is too sensitive. He never minds when someone teases or pranks his sister but when it comes to losing her, he gets concerned.

And he is not into sports too because he thinks sports makes a person more aggressive. I don't know what makes him think like that!!

I signaled Ethan to search around.

Jackson was so desperate to find his sister. I didn't know what to do, So I tried calming him.

"Um.. Hey Jackson we will definitely find her don't worry, okay?" I said trying to relax him.

"But what if she too disappeared like the rest" he said trying to fight back his tears.

I could easily see that he was fighting back his tears!!!

So I just gestured Ethan to take care of Jackson.

I made a quick move and started searching near the hill below.

Already an hour has gone by but she was still missing. So we thought to go back all the way down. It took us 20 minutes to reach the surface and we found Addison laying down over there **injured**!!

We swiftly ran and lifted her. Seems she was fully thirsty, Jackson quickly took the bottle from the bag. She gulped water in a single stretch and we all felt bit relaxed.

"Addison how come you ended up down the hill?" Jackson asked in a concerned voice.

Then she narrated...

"I was *walking* with you guys and I felt someone pulled my leg underground. When I looked down I could see a hand tightly clipped around my leg. I yelled and screamed but till then you were already half way up so you guys weren't able to hear me and then here I am laying down" she stammered.

"Who pulled your leg?" Jackson worriedly asked.

"As and when I screamed the hand which clipped my leg disappeared" Addison innocently said.

As she was badly hurt in her leg, three of us carried and took her to my home cause that one was the closest and we have first aid since my dad is a doctor.

She had sprained her leg, so we applied bandages but still she won't be able to walk on her own, she definitely would need support so I accompanied her.

We then suddenly heard a sound and we jolted and rushed towards the window.

We then noticed a stranger, smiling at us. We were horrified.

We burst through the door and looked around but there was no one. Suddenly I felt a cold gust of wind on my back and when I turned back I could see her!!!

The woman in white dress with a long hair. Our eyes met and she hurriedly aimed at us and asked in an ugly voice.

"Where is it?! Where is it?!

CHAPTER ONE

It was a very boring day in school just like any normal day, with umpteen HomeWorks.

Why do they make us suffer?! We have the right to deserve freedom, Don't we ?!!

Fortunately we have Field Day tomorrow, the best day for me as I love sports so much because:

- You don't have any homework to do in sports (duh!)
- Sports is my favorite and running is my thing..
- Sports is the only place where I win trophies and medals.

So these are the apt reasons why I love sports.... But let me tell you something, my little brother is total opposite to me,

- He is a Nerd
- He hates sports (definitely because he is last in it)
- He is always the TEACHER'S PET

These are the reasons I hate him so much and just because he gets good grades than me doesn't mean that mom can love him more than me.

Piece of a advice to you : Never keep a nerd brother at your home because if you have one, you will definitely feel left out because my parents always say yes for everything he asks and when I ask something they deny it with a big NO which really gets me on my nerves.

So yes I was totally on schedule with my work (NOT), while I was doing my home works I slept, can you believe it?! The next thing I wanted was my teacher's dialogue "you are an irresponsible kid........" With no choice left I must go to school.

I went down to have my breakfast and Ethan was munching on food....

I asked Ethan "Why aren't you being a book worm like usually!?"

"Today is field day and I have read everything so far even next semester's portion" he said rolling his eyes.

I know Ethan is 2 years younger than me but it feels like I am ten years younger than him!! it's all because of his nerdy looks and "mister know it all."

He asks me something and when I tell "I don't know" he keeps going on and on about how important it is and at last he tells the same dialogue.

"You know what Audrey? you have to focus more on studies and general knowledge."

Like who even asked him as I am already suffering with my syllabus and he is telling me that I should focus on **General knowledge?!!!** I won't listen to that little pesky brother of mine.

Anyways, I didn't want to spoil my day so I quickly had my breakfast and headed towards school. Ethan and I walked in complete silence which sometimes made me doubt if he was even walking with me.

It was a 5 minute walk to school and once we reached, I spotted my friend Addison. She has a twin brother and they both look alike, except she is a girl and Jackson is a boy (obviously).

Addison and me are like totally the same. We both love sports and running is our thing and yes, we both are of same height except she has blue eyes and I have brown but still we both have similar personalities.

“Wow Audrey this is the first time you are early to school” Addison sounded excited.

“Yes, how could I be late on field day?” I replied with a smile ear to ear.

The participants are the lucky ones as they don’t get to do anything, happy that I’m one of them, only the other students in our school have to arrange the seats, measure the starting and the ending points and coordinate all the activities.

What we as participants do is sit and relax (actually we warm up). So that means we are the chill out dudes. Addison and myself were doing some stretches when the volunteers came into the classroom and said that we participants should be there in 20 minutes.

I did some more stretches and joined Addison.

Mom and Dad were already seated in the second row with a very excited smile which gave me more confidence.

It was the Green VS Red team...Addison and myself were in green team, we went and joined the participants.

CHAPTER TWO

"On your marks, Get Set, Go" said Mrs. Olivia.

I was speeding up and up, the finish line looked like it was centimeters away.

Then with all the stamina I had, I jolted forward and crossed the finish line, Addison was right behind me so she was the runner up.

Next up was long jump which I am seriously good at.

Addison didn't participate in long jump instead she took part in high jump which is a bit hard for me, so I didn't consider joining it.

Well I aced at long jump and running so I got two prizes..... YAY I am so happy!!!!!

I can witness the happy smiles on my parents face and we waved at each other.

We all were then asked to get freshen up for the prize distribution.

I got ready and was waiting for Addison. We then merrily went and joined the queue to grab our awards.

"Audrey" my name was announced and I quickly ascended the stairs. I was about to trip if Addison didn't give me a supporting hand. I would have got embarrassed in front of the whole school, I owe her one.

I got my trophy and I carefully (without tripping again!!) descended the stairs.

After the prize distribution, I packed up my stuff to proceed home.

Then we heard an announcement, it's Mr. Harold our Principal announced "Dear students, don't be in a hurry we have a small announcement and a speech and that'd be the end of the event, I hope to see every one of you over there"

"And yes, all your parents can proceed to home," he continued.

So I went to see mom and dad before they leave.

I handed over my trophies to Mum.

"We are so proud of you Audrey!" Mom said happily.

"Thanks mum, If you guys don't mind I gotta go for an event. I am so sorry" I said trying to be on time for the speech.

"Yeah, yeah dear go ahead we'll see you at home" Dad said (trying to sound responsible).

"Yeah see you guys at home, love you, bye mum and dad" I replied jogging away.

CHAPTER THREE

"So dear students, Do you all know why we are here?" Mr. Harold said in a loud voice.

Mr. Harold motioned Amber, the most popular girl in our school, ascended the dais steps. She excels at studies and I bet there isn't a single teacher who won't stop praising her.

Addison and I exchanged dirty looks and were trying to maintain our posture as if we were keen listeners.

Speeches are the worst, It's just sitting and listening the lengthy speech. Addison and myself were engrossed thinking of the next year field day.

Amber with a pleasant voice started. "Good Evening Everyone...." She was interrupted by Mr. Harold.

"Hang on Amber" Mr. Harold said.

"We have a new student from 8th grade, let me take an opportunity to introduce you all"

Mr. Harold proudly announced.

We all were excited to know who it was!!.

After a thrilling suspense principal announced the name "Violet" and pointed towards her.

Our gaze turned towards her and seemingly she was like 3 inches shorter than me.She looks charming with blue eyes wearing an yellow top with blue jeans. She hails from Australia (that's what Mr. Harold said) I hope we can meet her after the speech...

Violet and Mr.Harold

Mr. Harold then gestured Amber, she continued the speech and it ended up with a big round of applause.

Seems the lengthy speech reached it's climax, finally we all were supposed to be dispersed and yes we all had rest of the day off.

We were heading towards the changing room and then Mr. Harold along with the new student Violet directed Addison and myself to tour the school.

Mr. Harold knows us well since we have actually helped him to find his favorite mug and we have been his favorite students ever since.

It went like this...

We had a substitution class and Mr. Harold was our substitute.

He seemed very sad, so Addison and myself were keen to know and we asked "what's bothering you Mr. Harold?"

"It's not that important to you students" he resonated.

"When you are bothered we won't leave you till you reveal the reason" I said confidently.

"I lost my favorite mug" he said seeming very down.

Addison rolled her eyes wanting to say "Who would cry over a lost mug?"

I scoffed wanting to say "I know right"

"Are you talking about the cup which had the text engraved "Best teacher" ?" Addison asked.

"Yes!!! Do you happened to see it?" He asked excitedly.

"Well it's not with me, but I saw you keeping it in your cupboard with the rest of your books" She said.

Mr. Harold hurriedly reached the cupboard and it was like a treasure hunt.

Finally he found it which was hidden behind the fat books.

From then on we were his dearest students.

Mr. Harold left and Violet followed us.

"Umm.. hey guys, I am Violet and I think you guys already know about me"

"Oh! Hi Violet, Nice to meet you" Addison and myself coincidentally greeted.

"Hey Violet, Don't mind me but I'm in love with your blue eyes." I said hesitantly looking at her eyes.

Violet grinned and replied "Thanks a bunch. I'm sorry but I do not know your names"

"Oh yes we totally forgot to introduce ourselves, This is Addison and I'm Audrey"

"Nice to meet you guys" she replied.

"Would you like to have a school tour now? Or can we do it tomorrow?" Addison questioned.

"We'll better have it tomorrow, I'm tired" Violet answered.

We then waved at each other and were making a move.

"Oh ok, So where are you guys heading now? Can I join you guys?" Violet asked.

"Actually we were heading to Audrey's home since I have some of my stuff over there" Addison replied.

"Violet I was just wondering, if you would like to join us?" I casually asked.

"You know, my home is nearby and I'm starving we can munch on snacks" I said patting my stomach.

"And since it's off for the rest of the day we can chat and get to know each other?"

"Wow, Sounds cool.. if you guys just wait for a sec I could dial my mom and let her know that I am visiting a friend of mine"

"Ok sure" I said.

CHAPTER FOUR

Violet convinced her mom for about 5 minutes and finally her Mom agreed with the plan.

I was excited, having a new friend come over, how cool is that?!

Three of us were heading out of the room then Addison reminded me about Ethan!

I totally forgot that I had to pick him up on the way to home, that little brother of mine is a severe headache.

And then Violet gave me the best idea ever!!!

“Hey! Jackson knows the way to your home right? Then why don’t you ask him to drop your bro?” Violet said.

Are you wondering how Violet knows about Jackson? Well that’s the power of friendship. In a short span of time Addison told ‘bout her brother.

“OMG!! Violet you are genius!!!” I said.

“Wait a sec I’ll go inform my brother” Addison swiftly took a move.

“That’s so sweet of you Addison” I winked and said.

“Addison and Jackson are the best siblings” I’d say.

Unlike Ethan and Me, they are like one in a million they never had a tiff. Wondering why?

So it all started like this,

When they were 5 years old they constantly quarreled just like any other siblings. But one fine day Jackson and Addison were in a world war mode, throwing stuff ,whatever is handy at each other and accidentally Jackson threw glass which hit Addison right on her head.

She was badly hurt and hospitalized but fortunately she recovered soon.

Jackson felt very sorry for his sister and decided never ever they should fight. Addison too promised.

And from that day onwards they are like **Made for each other** not **Mad for each other**.

So let me not drag further...a moral-full flashback isn't it?

That's the deal between them and they obey each other.

Sounds good Isn't? And that's the little tale behind these lovely twins!! I gave a brief explanation.

"So Violet do you have any siblings?" I asked.

"No I don't" Violet replied.

"OMG Trust me you are the most luckiest person!!! Believe me or not!" I eagerly said.

"Really?" Violet giggled.

Violet and I were involved in deep conversation.

And then Addison with heavy breathing came running to us.

"What happened?" I worriedly asked.

" Is Jackson picking up Ethan ?" I inquisitively asked.

"Yeah he is, But.." with a long breathe Addison paused.

"Addison what happened? Talk to me" I asked little worried.

"Umm.. your brother Ethan was missing in the class" she said gasping.

I was horrified,

"Are you joking?" I said hysterically.

"Jackson and myself enquired with his friends seems he already left home with one of his friend." Addison sympathetically said.

"They told what? Tell me!!!" I asked eagerly.

"They said that, He left home with his friend" stammered Addison.

"That little worm!!!! Such a mischievous fellow, look what I am going to do when I get home!!!" I screamed.

I stomped from the room exit, Addison and Violet followed me.

"How to calm her?" Violet whispered.

"Hold on...She is ferocious and in the verge of despair," she mumbled.

"Let's be with her and that's the only help we can do as of now" Addison said trying to be mature enough.

My subconscious mind overheard their conversation.

In about 5 minutes we reached our home, I burst through the front door and was hoping to see my parents but I couldn't see them.

"Mom, Dad are you guys home?" I anxiously screamed.

But there wasn't any response.

"Audrey I think your parents have gone out" Violet calmly said in a lower voice.

"Might be, But where is Ethan? Where did he go" I shrieked.

My parents will have me grounded if I lost him!!!!

"He might be at his friend's home" Violet said.

"Let me dial his friend" I quickly checked my phone and was running through his huge friends list..."

"It's Oliver" Addison said in a jiffy.

I kept scrolling through my phone but I didn't find the contact number!!!

"Guys I don't have his number" I said.

Then I heard someone open the front door.

CHAPTER FIVE

OMG

It was Ethan, I felt Happy and angry at the same time, But I felt that I would show him my angry side!!

"Where on Earth were you" I screamed.

"I...I... I was" Ethan stammered.

"Tell me before I lose my temper" I yelled.

"You have already lost your temper" He arrogantly replied.

I was left speechless.

"You..You... How dare you" I spluttered.

"Well I went with Oliver to his home as he bought a cool new fish called Betta.

You won't believe me, it's a fighter fish with a wavy tail, even it recognizes it's owner...

so unique isn't it? " He replied totally ignoring that I was angry.

"Well you could have told me right?!" a smile appeared on my face.

I then went and hugged him but look what he does,

"Umm Audrey can you stop squeezing me, I am kind of suffocating. It's not like I have been missing for months" He squeaked shaking me off.

"Ok, ok mister know it all.." I giggled.

"Going forward keep me informed where ever you go" I warned him.

Then I heard a squeaking voice.

"Umm Hi Ethan" I heard a kiddish voice.

I turned back and found it's "OLIVER"

"Hello Oliver" I gestured him to come in.

"Hi, I came to visit Ethan" he said.

"Why not?" I directed him to Ethan's room.

"Do you want some pan cakes?" I asked.

"I'll help you with it!" Addison joined.

"Thanks" Oliver headed towards Ethan room.

"Ok girls, lets head to my room" I announced.

Believe me or not Addison really nailed at preparing pancakes.

Oliver and Ethan were too engaged and having fun!!! I was surprised to see Ethan play as he always keeps his head buried in books.

My inner me thanked Oliver.

We were engrossed in our conversations.

I randomly looked at the clock, it was 8:30PM!! My parents were still not home. I was worried.

"Hey Audrey, I gotta go, I promised my mum that I will be back soon" Violet said.

"Yeah sure!" I replied.

"Hey Oliver? Do you want me to drop you?" Addison asked.

"That's so nice of you Addison" Oliver replied.

So Ethan and Me waved at them.

"Phew! That was awesome! I am tired" Ethan said exhaustedly.

"Ethan..." I said sheepishly.

"What?" He shrugged.

“Have you wondered something, I think this is the first time you ever had this much fun” I giggled.

“Really? You think?” He raised an eyebrow.

“Cuckoo.. Cuckoo” The Clock hummed.

CHAPTER SIX

We have a Cuckoo clock, It's like an alarm in our family. As and when the clock ticks 9PM, it means bed time...

"It's 9 PM! and still mum and dad have not returned" Ethan said timidly.

I convinced him somehow trying to be brave enough.

"Umm... yes. You know what? Let me dial in Addison and check if she dropped your friend Oliver safely. I said trying to distract him.

The phone conversation:

"Hey Addison did you drop Oliver?" I asked.

"Y---E---S" She said but her voice was breaking.

"Hey your voice is breaking" I sighed.

"W----H---A---T?" She Stammered (Well not really, I heard her stammering)

"Poor girl seems bad network", I thought.

"Hey! Do you have proper network there?" I yelled.

"I-----S---A----W-----S---O---M---E---T---H---I---N---G" She screamed.

"What???---"

'Beep...'

The call got disconnected.

I was bit worried, I didn't know what she saw! What if something terrible happened? I was completely lost in thoughts.

"What happened? Did she drop Oliver?" Ethan interrupted my thoughts.

"Yes, She dropped Oliver. But.." I paused...
"She said she saw something" I added.
Knock.. Knock..."I think it's mum and dad" I expected.

CHAPTER SEVEN

I opened the door my thoughts were shattered.

"Hey Audrey, is Addison with you?" Jackson asked.

"Shouldn't she be at home?" I doubted.

"She even dropped Oliver on her way home" I added.

"Umm.. Oliver who?" Jackson looked confused.

"Oh it's Ethan's classmate" I replied.

"Ahem.."

"He is not my classmate, He is my friend" Ethan rolled his eyes.

"Whateverrrr... Classmate or friend both are same" Jackson rolled his eyes.

"Yes true" I giggled.

"As if" Ethan muttered under his breath.

"Oh wait I forgot, I came here for another reason too" Jackson said.

"What's that?" I questioned.

"My parents are not at home I was wondering to know their whereabouts." He worriedly said.

"My parents are not home too" I sighed.

"Whatttt" he said.

"What, What?" said a voice behind Jackson.

"It's Addison" I was totally confused.

"What happened to your mobile" I assertively asked.

"Omg tell me what you saw? Are you even okay? Did you get yourself in trouble?" I kept questioning non-stop at her.

"Agghhh wait! stop shotting me with these many questions" She said drowsily.

"What? What did you see? Where did you see? Who did you see?" Jackson incessantly questioned with confused looks.

"Wait! Don't block my Oxygen guys please." She replied exhaustedly.

I know we were like the bad cops and were interrogating her. As if she did a HUGE crime.

"Umm do you want some water?" I asked shakily.

"Yes please, Oxygen with Hydrogen will absolutely help me out" she said sarcastically.

"She's got humor" Ethan replied giggling.

CHAPTER EIGHT

"I think this is the perfect time to tell what I saw" Addison replied taking a sip.

We were all ears.

"I dropped Oliver and while I was heading home I saw a ball moving on it's own, It was being passed left to right then right to left" Addison narrated the whole thing.

Jackson first chuckled then covered his mouth with his hands and he literally fell down and roared with laughter "You saw a ball moving on it's own?! Oh no there is a ghost playing with a ball" He sarcastically said.

I believe in ghosts and dark stuff trust me, I have an Ouija board.

You would have seen kids asking a pony or a princess dress but in my previous birthday I asked my parents for Ouija board and THEY ACTUALLY GIFTED ME ONE.

When I was 8 years old I asked for Annabelle the doll. As strange as it may seem, my parents didn't find a spooky doll so they bought a pretty doll and transformed it as Annabelle (I should tell, My parents tried their best to make it look like an actual Annabelle doll).

Me having an Annabelle and Ouija board is pretty cool because my brother doesn't snoop around my room cause he is scared of it!!.

Every one of us giggled.

"Tell me a bit more about what you saw actually. Did they look like they were kicking it or was the ball being passed through their hands?" I further probed.

"I don't care about Jackson at least my friend is believing me" Addison showed a face to Jackson.

And within seconds they both started teasing each other.

I had to break the 'Teasing contest'.

"Jokes apart" I screamed.

"Your friend is loud" Jackson said.

"Stop screaming " a voice from the other room.

Oops! I again forgot about Ethan.

"He would probably be buried in books" I firmly said.

"Wait what? How come he can study, when we all are in dire circumstances" Addison asked with her eyes wide open.

"I know right!!!"

I then had a big smile on my face "Addison are you thinking what *I am* thinking?"

"Am I?" She said smirking.

"Oh I know you are thinking about it" I grinned.

"Would you guys mind to tell us what you both are thinking about?" Jackson made us snap out of it.

"Well! Well someone wants to know what we are THINKING" Addison grinned.

"Addison and me are planning to use the....."

"OUIJA BOARD" We said in unison.

All of us went to my room since that's where the Ouija board was,

"Do you guys think it will work? Because I am 200% sure that there are no ghosts, Science says it all" Ethan poked his nose.

"Well science says that YOU SHOULD NOT POKE YOUR NOSE" Jackson said exhaustedly.

Oh God, Addison and me laughed so hard and we were seriously not able to breathe!!

I went and brought my Ouija board. It's been a while since I used it.

Addison blew the dust "Phew! That is so much dust, It is like a movie scene though"

"Yup I didn't use it because it was no more an exciting for me. It started to get boring, so I gave it a break" I replied.

"So you guys know how to use this?" Jackson seemed uncomfortable.

I scoffed "Duh!! Everyone knows how to play this"

We assembled the game. Though it took us sometime to drag Ethan.

To those who do not know what an Ouija Board is, here is a quick summary of "How to play" instructions.

Ouija Board

"If you've never used an Ouija board, the concept is pretty straightforward. With a group or by yourself, you place your hands lightly on a triangular pointer called a planchette. The planchette rests on the board itself, which has the words "yes" and "no" in it's top corners, an alphabet in the centre, and the word "goodbye" at the bottom."

So we spelled the word Ouija. We all had our hands on the planchette and started with some basic questions. First we asked if there is any spirit in this room and it showed,

"YES"

"No no no this is something fake there could be no spirits in here right?" Ethan stammered.

"Oh my god!! What is that? What is that behind you Ethan?" I shrieked.

"Wh-ha-at c-oul-d be th-ere" He stammered.

"NOTHING" I guffawed.

"Audrey!!!!! You know that I do not like when people make fun of me" He said annoyingly.

"I think that-----"

Whooooosh.... The curtain blew a gust of air.

I went to close the window but the window was already CLOSED!!!

"Guys the window is closed" I said trembling with fear.

"Ha Ha Ha! Oh my god I am so scared" Ethan laughed sarcastically.

"That's not funny Audrey" Jackson said.

"No wait, I remember I closed the window when Audrey, Violet and me were in this room" Addison uttered in panic.

We all were trembling then suddenly we were jolted by another...

"Coockoo..Coockoo"

"Omg it's 12:00" I trembled.

"This is it, Let's go out and check where our parents are" Addison pronounced.

"Where would we go and search?" Ethan trembled.

"I have an idea, What if we climb the hill and see over there?" Jackson suggested.

"Why on earth should we go to a hill" Addison questioned.

"Cause that's where we can get a better view. Start thinking big, don't be so dumb" Jackson explained.

"You have no rights to call me 'dumb' Who the heck are you to call me one" Addison yelled.

"My gut tells me that his idea is a sound one" I clarified.

"Wow Audrey! You took his side instead of mine. Seriously what a great friend you are" She said sarcastically.

"Woah! I don't wanna be involved between you two, I just said what I felt was right" I replied.

At last Jackson won and we went on to climb a hill.

We sneaked out but it was dark, with all our might we decided to go finally.

We quickly grabbed the water bottles, Flashlights and few snacks to munch on.

We all were tensed but managed to not show up on our faces.

"Everything is packed right?" I asked.

"NO, No, not everything, pack this sanitizer and a tent and also Mosquito repellent spray" Jackson advised Addison.

Addison was getting exhausted.

"You can thank me later" Jackson smartly said.

Ethan was with Jackson cause he was scared, Addison was carrying our backpack and I was leading the way.

Ethan kept trembling and Jackson was relaxing him .

CHAPTER NINE

After 20 minutes

THE PRESENT

We were gasping for air, when we reached the top hill. We four were panting and exhausted.

I was searching for Addison to quench my thirst as the water bottles were in her backpack. That's when I realized Addison was missing. I was shattered when I realized it!! And I was trembling to tell it to Jackson.

"Umm.. Jackson I think we missed Addison while we were climbing" I said tremblingly.

"You are joking aren't you?! Where could she go? Should be here only lets search!" he

said in a shivering voice.

Jackson is not a person who can stay strong, he is too sensitive. He never minds when someone teases or pranks his sister but when it comes to losing her, he gets concerned.

And he is not into sports too because he thinks sports makes a person more aggressive. I don't know what makes him think like that!!

I signaled Ethan to search around.

Jackson was so desperate to find his sister. I didn't know what to do, So I tried calming him.

"Um.. Hey Jackson we will definitely find her don't worry, okay?" I said trying to relax him.

"But what if she too disappeared like the rest" he said trying to fight back his tears.

I could easily see that he was fighting back his tears!!!....

So I just gestured Ethan to take care of Jackson.

I made a quick move and started searching near the hill below.

Already an hour has gone by but she was still missing. So we thought to go back all the way down. It took us 20 minutes to reach the surface and we found Addison laying down over there **injured**!!....

We swiftly ran and lifted her. Seems she was fully thirsty, Jackson quickly took the bottle from the bag. She gulped water in a single stretch and we all felt bit relaxed.

"Addison, how come you ended up down the hill?" Jackson asked in a concerned voice.

She then narrated...

"I was *walking with* you guys and I felt someone pulled my leg underground. When I looked down I could see a hand tightly clipped around my leg. I yelled and screamed but till then you were already half way up so you guys weren't able to hear me and then here I am laying down" she stammered.

"Who pulled your leg?" Jackson worriedly asked.

"As and when I screamed the hand which clipped my leg disappeared" Addison innocently said.

As she was badly hurt in her leg, three of us carried and took her to my home cause that one was the closest and we have first aid since my dad is a doctor.

She had sprained her leg, so we applied bandages but still she won't be able to walk on her own, she definitely would need support so I accompanied her ...

We then suddenly heard a sound and we jolted and rushed towards the window.

We then noticed a stranger, smiling at us. We were horrified.

We burst through the door and looked around but there was no one. Suddenly I felt a cold gust of wind on my back and when I turned back I could see her!!!

The woman in white dress with a long hair. Our eyes met and she hurriedly aimed at us and asked in an ugly voice.

"Where is it?! Where is it?!

"Is this the one you were seeking for?" said a voice of a girl.

"Where are you? Give it to me" The women said.

We all were popping our eyes out of our head to see who it was.

The woman turned and took the ring from the girl and moved aside, it was "Violet".

"Now thee may ask what thee want and I will fulfill it" the woman said.

"Do you have any idea about our parents? " Ethan quickly asked her.

We all reiterated the same dialogue in unison.

"Here, take this book and say no one that I gave it to you" She quickly handed over a book.

"Take it, quick! I have to go before "HE" sees "Me talking to the humans" she said.

"He who--?" before Ethan could finish, that lady vanished into thin air!!!

"What. Just. happened?" asked Violet.

We all were wondering the same thing.

"Violet where did you find the ring and how did you get here?" Addison asked.

"My parents were missing as well, so I thought to come and check on you guys. On my way, I saw a ring on the ground and curiosity had me at it's best so I thought to add it to my collection of rings."

"Then I heard the lady asking 'Where is it? Where is it' so I thought she might be referring to this ring" Violet said.

And I ended up here," she added.

Jackson picked up the book which was dropped by the lady.

"Umm.. Guys how 'bout reading what's in it?" Jackson said pointing towards the book.

"Sure" Ethan replied.

We opened the book and flipped through the pages, It was all dusty and ancient kind of.

Jackson handed the book to me.

I started reading it loudly "When~"

"Shushhhhh. Read quietly else someone will hear us" Ethan said.

"Someone who? There's literally no one here" Addison rolled her eyes.

"I don't know, what if someone like that magical lady appears out of nowhere?" Ethan questioned.

I continued whispering "When the wolves howled and the dogs barked the HIM came.."

"You know that makes no sense right? Because dogs bark normally but I do not know about the wolves though" Ethan interrupted.

"Maybe who wrote this was bad at English" Jackson replied.

I continued again! "HIM comes once in a million years. When he arrives it is the rebirth of the underworld."

"It's confusing I don't understand who HIM is" said Addison who had been quiet from a long time.

Ethan snatched the book from me and turned to the last page of the book "The conclusion or about the author is normally at the end"

"Ethan this is not a normal book to have~"

Suddenly we heard loud chanting voices and we were surrounded with plenty of people.

"Guys look!!! I think that's the HIM ghost" I said inquisitively.

We didn't know who HIM was but everyone seemed to welcome him chanting some stuff.

HIM had a unicorn head with a single horn and blue eyes, his body looked like a human body but with a rainbow tail. He looked like a mythical creature. He had a face like a human, two eyes, one nose and a mouth but he didn't have any ears.

We were standing and then suddenly a person next to me started tugging my shirt and gestured us to chant with him.

None of us knew what the chant was so we were like

"hum hum hup hup hum hum hup hup"

This was the tune of the chant so we were creating our own lyrics.

CHAPTER TEN

We looked at HIM only to find HIM looking at US!

We were scared to death!.

"Those kids! They are not one of us, Are they?!" HIM shouted pointing at us.

"We don't mean any harm mister HIM" Violet said.

"HIM?! HIM who?" HIM asked.

"You! Isn't your name HIM" Jackson asked stuttering.

HIM scoffed "I'm the king of underworld! I am the one who turns the bravest into bits! I am Theods"

"Theods? Why does this sound so familiar" Ethan asked joining his eyebrows.

"Yes it does! Theós and hades. My name is made up of two words" Theods said.

"I know what it means- Theó is god and hades is underworld in Greek" Ethan replied excitedly showing off his IQ.

Uggh I hate it when people talk nerd stuff. Now we four look so dumb in front of them.

"Yes combining them both makes it as god of the underworld" Theods replied.

"I don't want to interrupt you but I have several questions running in my mind" I firmly said.

Theods pretended to be more attentive.

"First who was the woman in white dress whom we just met before your arrival and Why there are so many people here?"

"And why was a ball floating in midair earlier?" Addison asked impatiently.

"When we were sucked up from our universe some unwanted people escaped with us. The woman you saw was no ordinary she destroyed three planets and as a punishment I turned her into a rat.

There are no people here it's just Lisa, Me and 5 others from our universe. The people you see are just hallucination which I created because we all missed our people."

Well I probably think the flying ball might be a prank played on you by some of the kids who were sucked up along with us " Theods explained patiently.

"Wow" that's what I managed to say after a brief explanation.

"Well we are from a parallel universe..." Theods was interrupted.

"PARALLEL UNIVERSE EXISTS?!" Ethan asked excitedly.

I pinched him to let him know that we had more important stuff than knowing if it exists or not!

"Also this kid interests me" Theods said pointing Ethan.

"Are you both done with your nerdy stuff?" Addison burst out.

We were flustered!!!

I signaled Ethan and murmured he was talking to our rival.

That's when Ethan realized.

"I WAS SPEAKING TO OUR RIVAL!!? Oh my- Oh my I didn't realize it".

"Ethan you are right and this is what we were trying to tell you from a while" Violet sighed.

"Please continue Theods there won't be any more interruption from our end" I promptly said.

All the ghosts were watching us having a 'simple conversation' with their "God Of underworld".

"Where are our parents?" Jackson asked anxiously.

"Parents?.." Theods scoffed.

"This isn't the time or the place to engage in a war of words," Addison said glaring at him.

These twins try to sound brave while they are sweethearts from inside.

CHAPTER ELEVEN

"We were living our lives when there was a sudden portal which appeared out of nowhere which sucked up five kids. They were Lisa's friends and she worriedly jumped to rescue them. I didn't want them to be on their own so with no choice left, I joined Lisa," Theods said.

"Does that mean the people from our universe were sucked in the portal and are navigated to YOUR universe?!" Violet asked.

"Yes and we need your help to find the core reason for this portal destruction" Theods said worriedly.

"Why us? How did you know we were still in this universe and weren't sucked up?" Addison asked curiously.

"My daughter, Lisa saw you all and found out that there were few people who still exist on Earth. So we thought to get help from you." Theods replied.

"So you are not the bad guys?" Violet asked concerned.

"We aren't, we just want your help" a sweet voice said.

Then a girl from behind appeared. She looked just like Theods But with long hair.

"My name is Lisa" she said.

She was wearing a Blue top with jeans and had a small horn on her head.

"Okay if we are done introducing ourselves and stuff can we look out for our parents?" Addison sighed.

"That's such a sweet name but as Addison said I think we could start searching our parents and the missing people" Violet said in a charming voice.

"Let's begin the hunt. There is a secret tunnel down over here, where the magician will be residing. We could ask him about the portal" Theods directed us.

"If you knew where he resided then why didn't you go search for him by yourself? Like why would you even need our help?" Ethan asked.

"We could have gone on our own but since this is Earth, it's different. We won't be able to go through the tunnel without a human's presence, that's what makes the tunnel secure" Theods answered.

"What if the magician was sucked up too?" I interrupted Theods.

"He lives in the tunnel so he won't be sucked up I guess," Lisa replied.

"I GUESS? What do you mean by that?" Jackson asked distressed.

"It's better if we check it out once!" Theods replied.

"Theods chanted a magic spell and suddenly there was a portal".

"Woah! That's sick!" I was awestruck.

"Wait if you can summon a portal to a tunnel then you should be able to summon a tunnel to your universe right?"

"I wish that was possible but it isn't, no one can create a portal to another universe" Theods sighed.

"I'll get in first" Lisa said as she stepped inside the portal.

Jackson followed Lisa and everyone followed each other.

Audrey following Ethan

Once I stepped in, all I could see was darkness everywhere.

"It's too dark in here" Violet said.

"Patience" Theods replied.

The very next second the whole tunnel lit up.

Theods led the way,

We all followed his footsteps.

"Are we there yet?" Ethan asked.

"Oh God! Once he starts 'Are we there yet' he won't stop" I said.

"Yes we will be, very soon" Lisa replied.

Eventually we reached.

It was a booth and had a title "Magician's corner" it looked quite small.

Ethan, Jackson, Violet, Lisa, Addison, Theods and me went in.

"Rest of you guys stay here while we 7 check this place out" Lisa said.

They all nodded back in response.

CHAPTER TWELVE

"WELCOME TO THE MAGICIAN'S CORNER"

A man in a tuxedo said, with a French accent.

He looked French I couldn't surely say though. He was tall with a witch hat just like an old style magician.

"It's me John, I need your help" Theods said.

"Theods? The God of the underworld? What brings you here" The magician asked.

"We were sucked up through a portal and hauled over here and the people of earth were sucked up as well but they were dragged to our universe" Lisa replied.

"To make a long story short people got switched with respect to their universe" Ethan concluded.

"I knew this would happen someday-The magician was interrupted.

"What do you mean?? If you knew this would happen you should have stopped it right? Or at least you should have warned us about it" Jackson questioned.

"Dear boy, I am a magician and a fortune teller. I know the future but alas I don't know when it would take occur precisely

You see I'm completely disconnected with the outside world. I've lived all my life over here because of which I don't really know what happens outside"

"Oh that makes sense" Jackson said surprisingly.

"But why weren't you sucked up like the rest?" I asked.

"Child, the place I live has a powerful force which restricts evil magic and I believe the place where you stayed had similarforce which stopped evil lurking around. Let me tell you a bit of history, an ancient magician "Merlin"the greatest and most powerful sorcerer selected few places on earth where he used his greatest spells to make sure evil doesn't creep around" he replied.

"If he was the most powerful sorcerer why didn't he use the spell on the whole earth?" Addison inquisitively asked.

"His motive was to make world a place without evil. But death is inevitable even for the most greatest magician " He sighed.

"I have a book which I got from Merlin and I hope this should have all the answers you were seeking for"

"The book has navigation details and you just follow the directives" The magician added.

"Why don't you disclose the details?" I asked.

"I have never opened the book yet because if a magician opens another magicians book it leads to a huge catastrophe" He replied.

"Okay then, We'll be making our way out! Thank you John" Theods said.

"Happy to help My old friend" John replied.

We left the shop and waved goodbye to John.

"How do you know about this magician?" I asked.

"He once visited our planet as part of a test - Theods was interrupted.

"What do you mean by test?" Addison asked.

"While he was studying in a magicians school in order to get graduated they have to pass a test."

"The test is to visit another planet and John chose our planet, that's how we met" Theods added.

We all nodded our heads.

"Let's surf the book" Ethan excitedly asked.

"We will, Once we get out of this tunnel" Lisa replied.

In short span of time we were at the exit.

"let's open the book !" I said.

Theods offered the book to Ethan so he could read it.

Ethan opened the book,

The first page was scribbled in gold. As he turned the pages, they were sparkling like glitter.

I was completely into the book, never have I ever been this interested in reading a book.

"Woah!! Cool!" Jackson looked surprised. I could see the gold reflection of the book in his eyes.

"Here is the first thumb rule, We need to memorize some chants because it's clearly written that this book shouldn't be taken to magical places" I affirmed.

"We got two spells so any two of you could volunteer and memorize it" Violet said.

"Good idea! We need two people so Jackson and Lisa you both have to memorize these spells"

'Lash-man-thu-kha'

'Lachi-man-kathi'

"Guys discuss which one of you will memorize which phrase" I said.

"Okay Lachi-man-kathi I'll memorize this one and Jackson are you okay with memorizing the other one?" Lisa replied.

"Yea sure anything is okay" Jackson said.

"Why should you memorize when we can take this book with us?" Ethan asked.

.

"Dummy we can't... it's not supposed to be" I replied.

Ignoring him I continued-

"As per the map we shall head towards Lost city of Atlantis" I said.

"I'll open up a portal to Lost city of Atlantis right away!" Theods said.

"You think it's that easy?" Addison asked.

"Well there's nothing wrong in giving a try" Theods said.

He opened up a portal but there was some kind of shield which didn't allow us to enter through it.

"Well this explains that it isn't that easy" Violet scoffed.

I kept turning the pages and found a note.

"Guys look! here it shows how to enter the Lost city of Atlantis" I shouted.

Everyone looked at me.

"We shall take a boat from the harbor to reach the Lost city of Atlantis"

"Where is the harbor?" Ethan questioned.

I looked sympathetically at Theods.

Theods chanted a spell and opened a portal.

"Hurry up" Addison said.

"Let's all assemble at the portal ,we will be heading to the harbor" Lisa said.

We all followed her lead. She makes a pretty good leader!

We stepped in the portal and each one of us were pulled to the other side.

CHAPTER THIRTEEN

"This is the first time I am visiting a harbor! Let's hope I don't get motion sickness" Violet sighed.

"Don't worry you'll be alright! Even if you feel uneasy Papa will caste a spell on you and you won't feel like you are in a boat at all!" Lisa replied with a charming smile.

"Thank you Lisa!" Violet said.

"Okay!! So let's check if all are here! Jackson, Audrey, Violet, Lisa, Theods, myself and extra five people " Addison kept counting.

"Oh wait! We don't even know these five members and we didn't even introduce ourselves at all! And why do you people remain silent?" Jackson asked.

"They do speak and are speaking now too...They don't understand your language and that is what stopping them to converse with you people" Theods replied.

"Ooh! But what do you mean by 'Speaking now too'?" Jackson asked.

"In our planet we do not talk a lot ,we communicate through our brains. If I think of Alice in mind then Alice alone will be able to talk to me. And only I speak English in our planet as I had a friend from Earth who taught me the language of yours. In our planet we can learn a new language by just touching the opposite person but I didn't do that as I wanted to master it through hardship and without an easy way. My papa here learnt this language by just holding me" Lisa explained.

.

"Woah! That's cool!!!! I would love to know the science behind this phenomena" Ethan said surprisingly.

"Well little boy with big glasses, it's all magic there is no science behind this!" Lisa giggled.

"I am no LITTLE BOY! I am 10 and I'm a tweenager! And nothing is possible without science in"—Ethan was interrupted.

"Well we all aren't just gonna stand here and listen to you guys, we have a whole planet to save ya know???!" I said all at once without thinking!

Lisa rolled her eyes.

"I- I- didn't mean that way! I'm sorry Lisa" I replied sighing.

"Hey!! You actually helped me to get rid of him! else Ethan would have gave me an head ache!" Lisa giggled.

All of us giggled! Except Ethan.

Lisawinked at Ethan and he started laughing too!

"We need to hurry up!" Addison shouted.

CHAPTER FOURTEEN

We all hopped on the ship.

It was huge, We travelled in a cruise before but never in a ship! It was just like a pirate ship!

"Hey guys check this out! It has a small kitchen here!" Violet pointed out.

"We won't be needing that" Lisa said.

"What do you mean? It takes months to reach Atlantis!" Ethan said.

"Did you forget we've got magic? Papa can make us reach in 20 minutes I guess" Lisa replied.

"Ughh these two" I rolled my eyes towards Addison 'the only sane person in this ship'.

"ikr! Im bored- Lets go talk to those quiet kids instead of just wandering"

"That's an amazing idea!" I replied nodding.

We found them sitting on the other side of the ship.

We went closer and gave a high five to each one of them so they could understand our language.

"Hello, Nice to meet you! I am Rose" a girl younger than us said.

"Hi!!! We are pleased to meet you! How old are you?" Addison asked.

The girl had blond hair and was wearing a bright pink dress. She looked bright as the sun, my eyes couldn't take the brightness.

"I am 10 years old and these are my friends! We all were meeting up in the playground and suddenly we all were sucked up through a wormhole which appeared out of nowhere

along with King Theods and princess Lisa" Rose replied.

Addison and I exchanged looks and tried to reduce the negativity in the air.

"Oh that's sad.. Now let's continue with other's introduction" I said excitedly.

A boy in a green shirt and black shorts spoke up "I am Evan and I am 8 years old".

"Nice to meet you Evan!" Addison sounded engaged.

"Why aren't you all having horns and tails? I didn't mean to take the liberty, just asking" I said.

"Well horns grow at the age of 11 and tails at the age of 12 and only kids of fairy's have wings and it starts growing at the age of 13 they grow so quickly within months" a boy in blue shirt and purple pants with a cap on said without a pause.

"Oh wait! I am Brune and I am 11 years old. Since my mum and dad both are fairy's I don't have tail" Brune said.

"Thanks for enlightening us Brune" I replied.

"I am Halsey and I am 12 years old. Brune and I are siblings. She had light autumn colour hair with wisp bangs which made her look beautiful.

I always say Brune that he was adopted but he doesn't believe me!" Halsey replied.

"Don't believe her! she loves to annoy me" Brune said.

"My god! *giggling* This is the same situation between me and my brother except he is 10 years old" I replied laughing.

"Well I guess it was a good choice to make you all talk!" Addison said giggling.

"Now let me introduce myself, I'm Alice and I am 13 years old" Alice was a year elder than us. she had a horn just like a unicorn. She wore a less brighter outfit which matched perfectly with her violet hair.

"Oh Hi! Alice nice to meet you! Well I guess we are juniors to you" Addison guffawed.

"Looks like it" Alice replied giggling.

My attention drew towards Violet and Lisa who were engaged in the kitchen and Violet was animatedly teaching recipes to Lisa.

I turned to look what everyone were busy with.

Jackson and Ethan were keenly learning to operate the helm and Theods was focusing the speed of the ship.

I thought to get some fresh air but we weren't allowed...

No one was allowed to go outside as the speed was too high and it will be hard for us to breath.

All of us were sitting at the corner of the deck. There was a desk where all 5 of them sat and two chairs were placed where Addison and myself were seated....

"YA'LL WE HAVE REACHED ATLANTIS YOU ALL CAN COME OUT NOW"

Lisa used a loud speaker to inform us. We all head out of the ship.

We were surrounded with water on all four sides, not sure where and how to descend from the ship. On one side Ethan was on absolute mute as he didn't knew swimming.

CHAPTER FIFTEEN

"Do we have to dive now? Cause boy, We got no oxygen underwater for your kind information- " Addison sarcastically said.

"You do not have to worry about that. I'll use my magic and cast a spell on you through which you will be able to breathe underwater just like fishes" Theods replied.

"What are we waiting for? Let's dive!" Jackson said.

Theods murmured a spell under his breath and pointed his hands towards us.

"I don't feel any difference at all" Violet said.

"That's because you haven't dived yet" Lisa replied.

First one was Rose. She just jumped without even thinking.

"Hey wai- I was interrupted.

"It's okay don't worry we already have the power to breathe underwater" Halsey said.

"Oh I was scared for a minute" I scoffed.

"Okay! Halsey and I will dive now" Lisa said.

Halsey nodded in agreement.

Once they dived they showed an OKAY sign which meant the next two people can dive.

"Jackson and Brune it's you guys now" I said.

Jackson agreed and dived with Brune.

"Evan and Violet go ahead and show us an OKAY sign once you meet rest of them" Addison said.

Violet agreed and held Evan's hand.

I was looking at Theods who was sitting at the edge of the boat and looked a bit down.

"Audrey, Ethan and I will dive now but can you tell him to stop asking me questions regarding the temperature and density of the water?" Addison sounded annoyed.

"Ethan I know you are afraid of water but look Theods will help you out and you don't have to worry at all cause Addison on the other hand is a professional swimmer and she won't let you drown at all okay? You believe me right?" I asked.

"Yes I do but I am scared Audrey. Promise me you will never leave me alone" Ethan sniffed and wiped his tears with his sleeve .

"Why would I ever leave you alone? I would never do that!" I said.

Ethan came and wrapped his hands around me still sniffing.

"Look nothing will happen to you okay? Once you dive in I'll be right behind you. I'll be there kay?" I comforted him.

"Awwww! Soo cute! I wish I had a younger brother rather than having a sloth as my brother" Addison said.

"Oh God! If Jackson heard this you both would end up arguing" I said giggling.

"Okay now! Let's dive ..others would be waiting for us" Addison said.

"Don't worry you will be fine!" I said comforting Ethan.

Before he even replied Addison pulled his hand and they both dived.

"Audrey you go ahead and dive. I'll come next" Theods said.

That was the first time he took my name I guess.

"I know something is bothering you. What's it?" I asked.

CHAPTER SIXTEEN

"It's just that Lisa is going to visit another planet for an assignment and she has to rule that place for a month- I interrupted Theods.

"Wai- Wait ruling a planet is an assignment?" I asked surprisingly.

"Well since she will be an official princess by next year her teachers are expecting her

to excel in all the aspects by being a single dictator without anyone's support and see how best she can emerge as a strong ruler" Theods explained.

"Okay..... it's a good thing right? What makes you worry then?" I asked.

"Well, I don't think she will be able to rule since she is basically a soft hearted person and doesn't like violence. But peace won't be the answer all the time" Theods replied.

"Well if we look through your point of view you are right but you have to understand her situation too right? If you walk in her shoes, she is right... It's going to be only for a month, she will get to grips with the situation and advise the wrong doers and if they still continue she will know what to do" I pacified.

"Yeah, I guess you areright. Once she experiences it she'll be a new person with new ideas and different perspectives" Theods replied with a smile.

"And also, Thank you. You have lightened my heart" Theods added.

"It's okay, I'm glad that you've understood Lisa's situation. Now let's proceed they all might be waiting for us" I hurriedly said.

"Okay! Wait, stand still I am going to cast a spell on you"

"Oka- Wait! Did you cast spell on others? On Violet, Jackson, Eth-

"Yes I did it when you were asking Halsey to jump" Theods said.

"Oh okay"

I stood still and Theods signalled me with a thumbs up basically telling that he was done casting the spell.

"I'll dive first is it okay?" I asked.

"Yeah sure"

I dived into the sea and the view was beyond amazing, I saw rest of them waiting near a huge coral. I waved at them and headed their way.

I kept my mouth shut as I didn't want to swallow sea water.

Theods stood next to me and started talking. I was in a state of shock! Talking inside water?!

"You all can talk, you are under my spell" Theods said.

I opened my mouth very little to ensure if the spell would really work and it really did!! I felt as if I was on land and could breathe, Talk and do all stuff!

"This is against science! This is totally not possible!" Ethan kept nagging.

"Well, okay then papa will take off the spell and you won't be able to breath nor speak" Lisa said.

"On a second thought, I'll better remain shut" Ethan replied sarcastically.

"Oh God! That's an excellent choice Ethan! I hope you remain like that for the rest of the journey" Lisa replied with sarcasm.

Gawd these two started bickering again.

"Let's not waste the time guys, we got work to do" I said with a straight face.

"Okay! So we have to find the lost city of Atlantis and once we do, we shall spot a castle....Inside the castle we will find a treasure box where we should solve a puzzle.

Once we ace it a portal will be appear. We have to chant the two spells to unlock the portal and then we would be able to go to the other side and...." I stopped.

"Damn- wait for a second! We don't understand a thing, you better elaborate this briefly once we reach the castle" Jackson interrupted me.

"God- never mind, I forgot that y'all were dumb" I replied rolling my eyes.

"And yes! The puzzle and spell is all my theory it's not mentioned in the book" I added.

"So how does the place look like?" Violet asked.

"It's a monument more like a castle and I believe it should be nearby" I said.

"Oooh okay! So as I was...." I was interrupted.

"Found it!" Ethan said.

"Where? How? Lead us to it first" I said.

"Follow me.." He raised his eyebrow in confidence.

He directed us the way through corals and though we have the urge to touch them we didn't as they are fragile in nature and we don't want to stress them as they are already disturbed from climate change.

"Y'all- see this? These are finger corals and... STOP DON'T TOUCH THAT!! IT'S POISONOUS!" he shouted at Rose.

She was startled but she nodded in response and was off from the Sea urchin.

"That is a Sea urchin, it's poisonous.. stay away from that" Ethan felt relieved.

We kept following him and then, there it was! '**The lost city of Atlantis.**'

"This- this is beyond amazing" Violet said.

"I have never seen something like this" Addison said astonishingly.

"Woah!!! This is so cool!!" Jackson said amusingly.

Lisa and Theods were dumbfounded.

It was picturesque. It was a huge land with broken stones. There were so many ramshackle buildings, seemsworld existed here and people survived and looked like it was suddenly abandoned.

"You are welcome!" Ethan interrupted my thoughts.

"Well how did you find it?" Lisa asked.

"You know, with a little bit of science and my brilliant brain.. Wanna hear how I *actually* found it?" Ethan asked in his annoying voice.

"No! No one wants to hear your boring and dreadful explanation" Jackson sounded annoyed.

"Let's not beat around the bush. We still gotta find the castle" I said.

"That won't be necessary" Addison said pointing to my right.

We all turned to look at what she was pointing to.

"Good job Addison" Theods said.

"Thank you" She said with a bunny smile.

"That was quick. Well now everyone follow Addison as she will lead us there" Lisa said.

"As if! I know stuff more than her. She thinks she is more intelligent" Jackson muttered next to me as we were following Addison.

"Jackson, stop whining! You're not a kid anymore" I rolled my eyes.

"First, I'm not whining! Second, why can't you just ignore it?" Jackson whispered.

"I'd rather go bang my head than talk to you" I had the sudden urge to punch him.

Jackson said something to me but it was barely audible, I thought it's better to ignore.

"Here we are!" Addison said breaking the tension.

"Woah! This looks just like Incan temple" Ethan said surprisingly.

"Inc.. What?" Jackson asked.

"Better don't ask him, he gonna give you a long explanation where you don't understand a single thing" I interrupted Jackson.

"Sharing is caring and I don't mind if you listen to me or not, as a brainy it's my responsibility to stuff your brains with information" Ethan said.

"So the **Inca** began as a small tribe who steadily grew in power to conquer other peoples all down the coast from Columbia to Argentina. They are remembered for their contributions to religion, architecture, and their famous network of roads through the region. Inca Temple is also one of the Wonders of the World" He added.

"Wow! This is the first time in forever I actually understood what you said!" I whispered with a 'how is this possible?' look.

"I know right! I'm impressed" Jackson agreed.

"Well sometimes I turn out to be wonderful you know?" Ethan said proudly.

"Only sometimes" I muttered.

"Let's get inside" Lisa interrupted our discussion.

We all entered at once, such a humongous entrance!

"That's sick!" Jackson said wowing the palace.

I was left speechless!

The palace was all white, whiter than anything I have seen so far. The walls were covered with white marbles and the floor was shimmering. The walls had a smooth texture, it felt unreal!! A place like this exists underwater!!.

We all looked up and it was majestic! It had the huge Chandelier!

"I bet this is more bigger than the largest chandelier located in Oman!" I said.

"Woah! You read about that? I thought you were a raccoon with no brain" Ethan replied in a mocking voice which really gets me on my nerves.

"WHAT DID YOU SAY?" I could feel my cheeks turning red, never have I ever been insulted this bad.

"Ah! Nothing, I just said I was impressed" Ethan changed his tone.

"Someone just kidnap him" I murmured under my breath.

"What was that?" Ethan questioned me with his eyes wide open.

"Oh I was just talking to myself" I replied with a sigh.

CHAPTER SEVENTEEN

"So we gotta find a treasure box which is most likely to be located in a hidden room." I commanded.

"But is there any clue? Or something? You know, to find the hidden room" Addison asked.

"I have no idea even I'm clueless" I replied.

"Theods? Do you know anything regarding this?" I asked him.

"I'm sorry, I'm unaware of the hidden room that you speak of." He said disappointedly.

"So we have no leads right now, we have to follow our instincts and try to find a hidden door to a hidden room" I said exhaustedly.

I could see Ethan heading towards a book shelf and I immediately knew what Ethan was going to do.

"Don't take that book!! Do you badly want to read now? seriously?" I asked sighing.

"Ethan! Pull the book! Do it!" Lisa said.

I looked at her perplexed.

Ethan stared at us blankly. He then pulled the book slowly and the book shelf creaked and revealed a room.

All of our faces were mixture of surprises and confusion.

"What do you think 'bout it ?" Ethan boasted.

"I thought this was just in movies" I said still trying to process the reality.

"Well? What are we waiting for? Let's get in!" Addison said.

"I'll go first y'all follow me " Lisa said.

"I present you the 'Treasure Chest'." Lisa said excitedly.

"Let's open it!!!" Jackson said.

I looked at the chest box but alas, it had a lock on. The smile on my face quickly faded away.

"It needs a key guys" I said sighing.

"How 'bout some magic?" Theods intercepted.

"Purr-fect!" I said giggling.

Theods casted a spell and the latch popped off.

I went closer to the treasure box and tried opening it but it didn't budge to open a bit.

"It won't open!" I said.

"Wait! Do you remember the spells? I guess those could be utilized now" Violet suggested.

"Oh god yes!! You're a smart cookie" I said.

"The chest is all yours now" I said looking at Lisa and Jackson.

"Lachi-man-kathi" Lisa spelled.

"Lash-man-thu-kha" Jackson looked nervous than ever.

The way he pronounced made us all burst out laughing!!!

He hid his face in embarrassment.

"Ah! It's ok. You tried your best" Violet said.

Addison scoffed.

The treasure chest opened revealing a small box.

"Lisa open it!" I said.

"Me? Why?" She looked surprised.

"Cause you are the 'to be princess' and more like the leader of this crew" I said giving her a comforting smile.

"Well! That's so kind of you!!" Lisa replied.

She held the box in her hand and opened it. We could barely see what's inside.

She found a piece of paper, held it up to make sure it's visible for everyone.

"It's a spell I guess?" Addison said warily.

"It is and we have to make sure we make no mistake in pronouncing it" Theods said.

"Well Lisa can do it with ease!" I said looking at her.

"Wish me luck guys!" Lisa looked thrilled.

"You'll do it don't worry" Violet said.

"Don't be such a baby! Do it already!" Ethan said.

"I AM NOT A BABY" Lisa said Annoyedly.

"Well then do it already!" Ethan said.

"Jackson, do you wanna say something?" Addison said giving a glare to Jackson.

"Ughh! Do I have to? Well, All the best Lisa You can do it!" Jackson said sarcastically.

"That's more like it" Lisa said giggling.

Lisa cast the spell which I wasn't able to understand a bit.

Our faces went blank since nothing changed after her spell..

"Nothing happened?" Jackson worriedly said.

"It will! Wait" I said.

And the very next second, a huge portal appeared in front of us. It looked completely different on the other side. The edges of the portal sparkled with fire.

I peeped through the portal and saw people just like Theods and Lisa and I turned right and found people of Earth!!!!

"It is the right portal! I could see the people of Earth" I said.

"Whaaa!!!" Everyone were murmuring and screaming happily.

"Ok so first! Rose, Evan, Alice, Brune and Halsey I want you five to enter through the portal!" Lisa said.

Lisa entered the portal and gestured the five to enter inside.

All the five hugged us we gave handshakes.

"We'll miss you a lot" Rose said with a comforting smile.

"If we meet again, I want you to share some tips to stop your brother from annoying you" Halsey whispered to me.

I giggled "Sure I would!"

"Ethan! It was fun meeting you" Brune said to Ethan.

Evan, Brune and Ethan had a group hug. Aww they looked adorable!!

"Well, junior see ya next time" Alice said giggling.

"Sure we will" I replied with a wink.

Alice, Halsey, Addison, Rose, Violet and I shared a group hug and waved each other goodbye.

I saw Theods getting inside the portal and I said him a sincere 'Thank You'

"Meet you next time Audrey! And yes thanks for the advice" He said.

I smiled.

"Lisa, you are going to be a wonderful princess!!! You have all the qualities" I said hugging her.

She hugged me and waved at us and stepped on the other side of the portal.

"Also yes! I will open up a portal where you all will be directed to your homes" Theods said.

As he was leaving, he casted a spell and a portal emerged on my right.

A lot of people kept coming out of the portal. There were many people from our town and a few I couldn't recognize. After I guess, half of our town's population came through, I could see my mum and dad hurrying out, Ethan and me rushed to them and hugged each other.

Mom and dad coming through the portal

Ethan was so busy asking stuff to mum and dad that those three forgot I existed.

I was checking the portal if people were still coming and suddenly I felt something below my shoe, I looked down and there was a note.

I picked it up and it read;

'Beware, I will be back soon and capture Theods and be the new King'

I was horrified, who could this be? And why would that person do this??

I tried to show the note to Theods but the portal had already closed. Not knowing what to do, I slipped the note inside my pocket and I got back to my parents.

We all, along with our parents entered the portal and once everyone did, it closed automatically.

CHAPTER EIGHTEEN

2 weeks later

"Ethan did you see my phone?" I asked whilst wolfing down my food.

"How'd I know??"

"I don't know, maybe because you keep snooping around my room!"

"Excuse me?"

"You heard me"

I gave up and headed to my room to find my phone.

It's been two weeks since the 'Earthling disappearance' event took place.

Everyone were shook by it and some are still trying to process the reality.

Whereas our family has been living like nothing had gone wrong,

Same day, all day.

I went up to my room and found my phone laying on the table. I went to the table to grab it and there was a note next to my device.

It read ***'I said I'll be back, didn't I? Well I am!'***

Note from Author.

I know I left you all with a dramatic suspense! But you readers know that I love to end a story with a cliff hanger! So now the story is yours to imagine!. What if and What if not? You have to answer these questions by yourself!! Well if you want another hair-rising story, Hang on till my next book is published. Till then Adios!!!!

9 798885 918916

Printed by Libri Plureos GmbH in Hamburg, Germany